DreamWorks
DRAGONS

How to
RAISE THREE
DRAGONS

adapted by Ellie O'Ryan

Hodder
Children's
Books

HODDER CHILDREN'S BOOKS

First published by Simon Spotlight
An imprint of Simon & Schuster Children's Publishing Division
1230 Avenue of the Americas, New York, New York 10020

First published in Great Britain in 2017 by Hodder and Stoughton

A CIP catalogue record for this book
is available from the British Library.

ISBN 978 1 444 93432 8

Printed and bound in China by RR Donnelley Asia Printing Solutions Limited

The paper and board used in this book are made from wood from responsible sources

Hodder Children's Books
An imprint of
Hachette Children's Group
Part of Hodder and Stoughton
Carmelite House
50 Victoria Embankment
London EC4Y 0DZ

An Hachette UK Company
www.hachette.co.uk

www.hachettechildrens.co.uk

Hiccup's new invention, the Thunder-Ear, was finally ready. He couldn't wait to test it!

Stoick had never seen anything like the Thunder-Ear.

"It can track dragon sounds from miles away," Hiccup explained.

Stoick leaned close to the Thunder-Ear.
He could hear Fishlegs and Meatlug
singing. But they were very far away.
It worked!

Then Stoick heard something even worse. "Tell them to stop singing," he said.

But the terrible noise wasn't Fishlegs and Meatlug. It was three baby Thunderdrum dragons!

Stoick's dragon, Thornado, was a Thunderdrum, too. He recognised their cries and zoomed off to find them. They were all by themselves on a sea stack.

Hiccup didn't want to leave the babies
alone. But Stoick said they were too loud
to live in the village.

"They'll be okay on their own," he told
Hiccup. "Thunderdrums are the toughest
dragons in the world!"

The next morning Hiccup jumped out of bed. What was that terrible noise?

It was the Thunderdrum dragons! They had followed Hiccup and Stoick back to Berk. And they were out of control!

The baby dragons zoomed through houses, crashed into food carts, and even scared the sheep!

"Can someone help me wrangle them into the Academy?" Hiccup shouted.

"I thought you'd never ask!" Astrid replied. The two friends worked together to catch the babies.

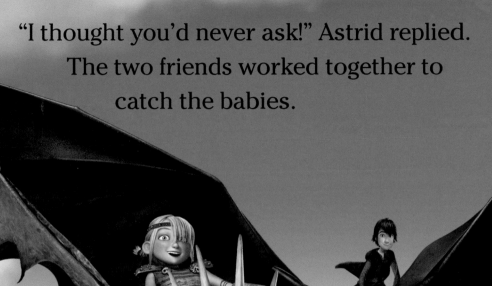

"Get those troublemakers off the island now!" Stoick ordered, once Thornado had calmed the three baby Thunderdrums.

"Don't you think we should train them?" Hiccup asked.

Stoick thought about it. Thornado was was a great dragon. Maybe the baby Thunderdrums would be useful, too.

Their training began at once.

"I guess the first thing we should do
is name them!" Hiccup yelled.

The Thunderdrums were so loud that
they drowned out everyone else!

The friends decided to call them Bing,
Bam and Boom. Noisy names for noisy
dragons!

At first Bing, Bam and Boom
did what Hiccup wanted. But
then the trouble started.

Bing, Bam and Boom roared so loudly that Hiccup flew across the arena.

When Astrid told them to stay, they flew in circles.

Snotlout set up some targets, but they knocked him down instead! They even swiped Fishlegs' sword!

At last the Thunderdrums were calm.

"We're finally getting through to them," said Hiccup.

But he was wrong. It wasn't the training that made the Thunderdrums behave. It was Thornado!

Bing, Bam and Boom were perfectly behaved with Thornado. They wanted to be just like him. And when Thornado flew out of the arena, the babies followed him!

"Close the gates!" yelled Hiccup.

But it was too late!

Once more Bing, Bam and Boom
raced through the village. They shrieked,
roared and wrecked everything!

"The Thunderdrums have to go," Stoick
ordered.

Everyone worked together to take Bing, Bam and Boom to a new home on Dragon Island.

"Here you can be as loud as you want," Hiccup told them. "It will be great!"

Then Hiccup, Toothless and the others flew away from Dragon Island.

Far below, the baby Thunderdrums looked as sad as Hiccup felt.

Back at the village Hiccup had a big surprise. Bing, Bam and Boom had followed him – again.

Stoick was not happy to see Bing, Bam and Boom.

"It looks like Thornado and I need to give you a hand," he told Hiccup.

Thornado led the baby Thunderdrums
back to Dragon Island. Hiccup and
Fishlegs followed on their dragons.

Hiccup said goodbye to Bing, Bam and Boom again. They started to cry. That made Hiccup feel even worse.

"Don't look back, son," Stoick said as they flew away.

But when Hiccup heard a scary roar, he had to see what was happening.

A pack of wild dragons surrounded
Bing, Bam and Boom!

"We're not going to let any wild dragons
bully our boys, are we?" Stoick yelled to
Hiccup's surprise.

Thornado and the other dragons raced
back to Dragon Island. Then Thornado
used his roar to scare the wild dragons
away. Toothless and Meatlug helped too!

At last the baby Thunderdrums were safe! But what if the wild dragons came back? Bing, Bam and Boom were too young to be alone.

Stoick knew what he had to do.

Stoick removed Thornado's saddle. "Take care of your new family," he said. "Goodbye, old friend."

It wasn't easy to say goodbye, but Stoick knew it was right. Thornado was a great dragon and now he would be a great dad!